This book belongs to:

Frank

A catalogue record for this book is available from the British Library

Published by Ladybird Books Ltd
80 Strand, London, WC2R 0RL
A Penguin Company

2 4 6 8 10 9 7 5 3 1
© LADYBIRD BOOKS LTD MMVIII
LADYBIRD and the device of a Ladybird are trademarks of Ladybird Books Ltd

ISBN-13: 9781846467967

Printed in China

my favourite
BEDTIME RHYMES

Illustrated by: Greg Becker,
Desideria Guicciardini,
Fernando Luiz, Anna Luraschi,
Tracy McGuiness-Kelly Advocate - Art,
Paul Nicholls Advocate - Art, Caroline Pedler,
Andrew Rowland Advocate - Art,
Katie Schaefer and Natascia Ugliano.

Wee Willie Winkie

Runs through the town,

Upstairs and downstairs

In his nightgown.

Rapping at the window,

Crying through the lock,

"Are the children all in bed?

For now it's eight o'clock!"

Rock-a-bye, baby, your cradle is green,
Father's a nobleman, mother's a queen.
Betty's a lady and wears a gold ring,
And Johnny's a drummer, and drums for the king.

Lullaby and good night, mummy's delight,

They will guard you from harms,

Bright angels around my darling shall stand.

You shall wake in my arms.
They will guard you from harms,

You shall wake in my arms.

Hey, diddle, diddle,
The cat and the fiddle,
The cow jumped over the moon.
The little dog laughed
To see such fun,
And the dish ran away with the spoon!

Twinkle, twinkle, little star,
How I wonder what you are!
Up above the world so high,
Like a diamond in the sky.

When the blazing sun is gone,
When he nothing shines upon,
Then you show your little light,
Twinkle, twinkle, all the night.

Niddledy, noddledy,
To and fro.
Tired and sleepy,
To bod we go.

Jump into bed,
Switch off the light,
Head on the pillow,
Shut your eyes tight.

Sleepy-time has come for my baby,
Baby now is going to sleep.
Kiss mummy goodnight
And we'll turn out the light,
While I tuck you in bed
'Neath your covers tight.
Sleepy-time has come for my baby,
Baby now is going to sleep.

Girls and boys come out to play,

The moon is shining bright as day.

Leave your supper and leave your sleep,

And come with your playfellows into the street.

Come with a whoop and come with a call,

Come with a good will or not at all.

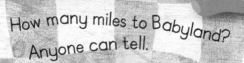

How many miles to Babyland?
Anyone can tell.

Up one flight,

To your right,

Please to ring the bell.

I see the moon,
And the moon sees me.
God bless the moon,
And God bless me.

Sleep, baby, sleep,
Your daddy keeps the sheep.
Your mummy guards the lambs this night,
And keeps them safe till morning light.
Sleep, baby, sleep.

Sleep, baby, sleep,
Down where the woodbines creep.
Be always like the lamb so mild,
A kind and sweet and gentle child.
Sleep, baby, sleep.

Come to the window, my baby, with me,
And look at the stars that shine on the sea.
There are two little stars that play at bo-peep,
With two little fishes far down in the deep,
And two little frogs cry, "Neap, neap, neap,
I see a dear baby that should be asleep!"

Golden slumbers kiss your eyes,
Smiles awake you when you rise.
Sleep, pretty darlings, do not cry,
And I will sing a lullaby:
Rock them, rock them, lullaby.

Care is heavy, therefore sleep you;
You are care and care must keep you.
Sleep, pretty darlings, do not cry,
And I will sing a lullaby:
Rock them, rock them, lullaby.

Hush-a-bye, baby,
On the treetop,
When the wind blows,
The cradle will rock.

When the bough breaks,
The cradle will fall,
And down will come baby
Cradle and all.

Star light, star bright,
First star I see tonight.
I wish I may, I wish I might,
Have the wish
I wish tonight.